It Might be Sunlight

Sonia Orin Lyris

Copyright © 1993, 2012 Sonia Orin Lyris

All rights reserved.

ISBN-13: 978-1480090316
ISBN-10: 148009031X

DEDICATION

To my fans who insisted I reprint this so they could have a copy. To Rolf, JC, and the rest of you -- you made this happen.

It Might be Sunlight

Light that might be sunlight comes from the room's many high windows.

I turn and look at this large, familiar room, the only sound the brush of my bare feet on cool marble. Round walls encircle me. Above is a dome, made of many windows. There are no doors.

I hug myself, to feel skin against skin. I scratch myself. I wear no clothes, but I am not cold. Not here.

The room smells of nothing. Or perhaps of dust.

I turn around and around, but there is nothing to mark one direction from another, except the light on the walls that comes through the high windows. The walls are white, the floor shades of grey. Through the dome windows I see a blue that might be sky.

Just like yesterday.

The air is quieter than the dreamless sleep from which I have recently woken. The silence fills the room, and wraps me as though in a silk cocoon.

Good morning, Kelly, he says.

His words do not disturb the silence. They come to me, like my own thoughts. Only different.

I nod.

I hope you had a pleasant sleep, he says silently, this one who I call Captor, and sometimes Tormentor. This, my only companion.

Is the sleeping supposed to be for my pleasure? I ask.

The question is slow; I have to hold it in my mind so that he can read it. It has been a long night since we last spoke. I have to remember how to do it.

Your pleasure, he answers, his crystal bright thought forming in what was an empty corner of my mind. *Yes. This is all for your pleasure.*

I shake my head. *Open the cage*, I say, *and let me out. Then I will have what pleasure is left to me.*

There are eyes in my mind now. Or maybe not, but that's how it feels. The eyes watch me and are sad. They blink.

If I let you free, you will perish.

I nod, unsurprised. We have had this conversation before.

Then he smiles into my mind. *Today* he says, his eyes wide and sparkling with anticipation, *today we will have many pleasures.*

How long, I ask, *since yesterday?*

The eyes close. I taste dismay.

That would only upset you, he says.

How long, I repeat.

I sharpen my determination, imagining my need to know as a hard surface around my mind, using my confidence to harden my resolve to know.

I do not want you to be upset, he says. *Are you sure you would not rather discover that today is your ninth birthday?*

Each time I wake he is more reluctant to give me a measure of the time passed. This time, like the last, he tries to bribe me.

Now he swims through my memories, each one brought alive by his touch.

Suddenly I am nine. I sit at a table with seven other children. I smell strawberries, cake, and vanilla ice cream. The memory expands until it is more vivid than my sparse present.

I cling to my anger at his manipulation, and he is momentary confused. We have no privacy, my former self and I, and he does not understand why I should resent his intrusions. He only understands that the memories affect me.

His reaction is to expand the memory until it fills me, until it entirely replaces my present. I struggle to remember that I am not nine. I slip.

My friends sit around me at the dining table. The blond boy at the end of the table is destined to be my lover some years hence, but I have no hint of that now. Or maybe I do. Maybe that is the soft whisper from the future that touches me when I look at him. Yes, I think it is.

Colored paper and ribbon are scattered over the table. Before me is the final gift, amazingly large, sparkling with mystery and promise. I start laboriously untying the knotted ribbon. With a roll of my eyes at my two closest friends, I yank off the ribbon, rip away the paper, and open the box.

Somewhere inside me is an echo of this moment, an echo that comes from the first time, when it happened. Now I do not remember what the gift was, but I remember that it will be wonderful.

I am standing again on grey marble, light coming down from the windows above. It is an advertisement, this memory. A promise, like the gift itself. All I have to do is agree to the offer.

I shake my head.

Christmas morning, then, he says. *You were eleven. Do you remember?*

I am at our old country house, and my bedroom looks onto the sloping field where wildflowers grow in the spring. It snowed last night, but today's morning sky is clear and gloriously blue.

I put my fingertips against the cold window and watch as the glass fogs around each finger. Outside, every tree is snugly wrapped in white, and the field has become a thick white carpet that waits for nothing. Except, perhaps, my boots.

An odd sound, a muffled squeak, comes

from somewhere in the house. My parents' hushed voices follow.

Warmth fills me from head to toe. It is a puppy. Asked for so many times, and finally here.

I dance across the room and dream of the games we will play together, my puppy and I, and the footprints we will leave together outside, in the snow of this perfect Christmas morning.

I am back in the domed room again.

I think of Shakti, who was my friend and companion for so many years. I see her face, I hear her bark. The memory makes me warm. I blink away tears.

All I have to do is agree.

No, I say, my mouth forming the silent word. Quickly, so that I will not change my mind.

A mirror, then, my captor says, trying a third time to tempt me.

Some long days ago my captor showed me a mirror. Understanding brushed by me like a breeze, hinting at the key to unlock my cage. Then he took the mirror away, and with it went my insight.

Even if the insight was illusion, I very much want to look in the mirror again. But I need to know how much time has passed while I slept.

How long, I ask. I try not to think of anything else. Not the gift, not Shakti, not escape.

My captor sighs in my mind, a long exhale of dark, dusty breath. Minutes pass; minutes, I am sure, because I count the seconds. I have reached three minutes and twenty seconds when the sigh finally ends.

I will tell you, he says. *But listen: these are days as your ancestors knew them, not as I know them. Not even as you know them now.*

You tell me this every time, I answer.

Yes, but I think you must not listen, because you are always dismayed when I tell you how long it has been.

Tell me.

A moment passes.

In the days of your ancestors, you have been asleep for ninety-eight thousand, seven hundred and twenty-one days.

Nearly three centuries. Even longer than last time. I feel numb shock, frustrated anger, then despair.

I look down at my hands, stomach, legs. I tell myself that this body is not mine, that I am no longer alive, that no one can live this long. The real me is dead.

He has withdrawn all but a tendril of himself from my mind. These emotions do not feed him.

No, he says, *you are not dead. You breathe and think. Sometimes you play. You are not dead.*

I look up at the windows above me, at rectangles and triangles of blue. Is it the blue of Earth's sky, of any sky, or only illusion?

Illusion? he asks as he frowns into my mind. *How easily you use that word. Does it mean so little to you that the food tastes good and fills your stomach?*

It is not enough that my stomach is full.
Perhaps if you were hungrier, it would be.
Hunger is something we both understand.
Perhaps, I answer.

This is also a conversation we have had before. I have already given the other answers that occur to me now, except the one he wants to hear, the one in which I accept his offer and lose myself to my best memories.

Come, he says, *today we will have many pleasures to explore. I am eager to begin.*

We have a fragile compromise; he constructs fantasies from my mind, and I tell myself that I do not live in my memories. It is a small lie, which neither of us believes. I know that it all comes from my past, whether the memory is an ice cream cone with chocolate sprinkles, or the summer night when my heart was broken into a million, sharp pieces.

Why do I sleep so long? I ask.

Sleep is for rest. You have to rest.

You don't rest. Why should I?

You are different. Very delicate. If you do not rest, your -- elements -- will not stay together.

My elements. Do you mean my mind?

Yes, your mind. But this is not pleasure. Let us have pleasure.

Your pleasure is not my pleasure, I say.

You are wrong, he says. I taste his arrogant certainty. *I know what your pleasure is.*

You don't. I want --

I feel him shake his head at me, and my forming thought pauses. This is my invention, that he has a head to shake.

Then he waves a hand across my mind, and my thoughts are washed away, sucked down like a sand castle under a retreating surf.

You don't know what you want, he says. *The freedom for which you lust would destroy you. If you are destroyed, the pleasure goes away for both of us.*

The words bounce around in my head, like pebbles in a tin can. I struggle to remember my thoughts of a moment ago.

Waves and sand castles. I'm not sure.

Come. I hunger for your pleasure.

Your hunger, I throw back at him, making the thought hard and sharp, *is not my problem.*

My anger confuses him. For a moment he withdraws, but then he is back again, rummaging through my mind for clues. He is at once an itch and an ache. I shake my head sharply, hoping to make the feeling stop. It doesn't.

He moves deeper into me, more quickly than I can follow.

A nightmare bubbles into memory. He sees the memory, enhances it, and I cringe as it becomes real.

I look down. There is a worm crawling around on my stomach, moving just under my skin, swimming through my flesh. I am horrified. I scratch and scratch until my skin breaks open, scratch the worm away with a bit of blood. It hurts, but the worm is gone. I am relieved. Then I look down again.

There are dozens of worms, just like the first one, wriggling in circles under my skin.

The dream ends.

I am standing on marble again, shaking. There are no worms, no blood.

I clench my fists. It is all I can do.

I dreamt that dream long ago, when I was back at the Institute, studying for the trip one of us would make to Epsilon Eridani. Back then, I could wake from my nightmares. And I slept for hours, not centuries.

My captor throws me a fuzzy sphere of anticipation. The smooth, curved wall around me blurs. Now there are doors. Many doors.

Look, my captor says excitedly. *Pick one.*

All the doors look the same. I take a few steps toward one and stop. With perfect, innocent cruelty, he adds, *If you pick the right door, I will set you free.*

It might be truth, so I play the game, even knowing that my hope feeds him.

I walk forward until I reach a door. I push. It swings open.

Inside is another circular room, just like the one I am in. On the other side of that room stands a naked woman who from the back looks like me, peering through an open doorway. I turn around and there she is again, just beyond a doorway across the room, looking behind herself.

You picked the right door, he says gleefully.

You are free. Go on, go in.

I feel a crushing pressure, which turns cold inside me. I abandon words.

I draw a picture of his face in my mind. It is my own construction, because I have never seen him. I twist the face. I pull it. I poke it. I drip foul-smelling green slime from its nose, and I rot the skin until it swells, blackens, and falls from the bones.

I feel his shock. He withdraws. I cannot keep the picture in my my mind, hard as I try, and it fades. It is a minor victory, but it gives me some satisfaction, some real pleasure.

He floods back into my mind, to drink in my pleasure. He must be hungry to take this little bit.

A bee feeds at a flower, a giraffe nibbles leafy foliage, a kitten chews on a piece of tuna.

I decide not to play. One step back and the door closes. Behind me I hear a door close.

You are not happy, he says. I hear his hunger.

No.

Why not. I will give you anything.

The conversation is a daily ritual.

Let's just say we have irreconcilable differences and get a divorce, I say.

He does not understand. With access to all my memories and centuries to digest them, still he does not understand.

You are lonely, he says.

I laugh. A breathy laugh; my voice is rusty from lack of use. It tickles me that it has taken him centuries to reach this conclusion.

Don't be absurd, I say, smiling. *How could I be lonely when I have you?*

He searches my memories to understand why my words and emotions don't match. He pushes and probes. I wince and shake my head.

He goes deeper.

No, I say, *don't* --

It is morning, a fresh, bright, brittle morning. I am waking up slowly, clinging to sleep. This morning, this day, the third day since -- no. I won't think it. Since -- no.

I roll over in the soft bed and pull the pillow over my head. I want to sleep again, I want to sleep forever, but I am awake now, abandoned by sleep to the sharp rays of sunshine that poke at me through the lacy curtains.

For a long time I stare at nothing.

The phone rings. I don't want to answer. I do anyway.

"Kelly? It's Roxanne."

Roxanne took Simon's cats when he came to the Institute. She brought them back when the Institute decided it was okay for Simon and me to live together, even though we were both candidates.

She is part-time support staff at the Institute, but no less eager than any of us to get someone to Epsilon Eridani, to find the intelligent life that sent us a list of prime numbers nine years ago.

"Oh, God," she says to me. "I just heard.

Kelly, I'm sorry."

I don't know what to say.

"Yeah. Thanks."

"Is there," she inhales, "any hope --?"

"No," I say. I've answered this one enough to make it a litany: "Massive injuries. Severed spinal chord. Brain damage. No chance."

She is silent.

I sound so clinical. That's good, I'm a scientist. My teachers at the Institute would be proud. Simon would be proud.

"The driver had a heart attack. Just like that?"

A perfect tragedy. Everyone a victim, no one to blame.

I blink. Slowly. Again. "Yes."

The Institute for Alien Studies made us into detectives. We learned to piece together a whole from any set of parts, or at least to construct plausible inferences for the data at hand. We didn't know what we would find at Epsilon Eridani, so the Institute prepared as best they could. I was ready for anything.

Except this.

Even so, my well-trained mind ignores my emotions. I recall the police report pictures, and I see a full-color simulation in my head. I try to turn it off, but I can't.

Simon leaves the corner store with two packs of bubble gum, a pack for him, a pack for me. I don't chew the stuff, but he still buys it for me. Sometimes when he snaps his gum and blows bubbles, I think I'll have to strangle him to stay sane, but I keep my silence under the flag of love. We all have our annoying habits. I chew through pens almost as fast as he goes through gum.

Simon steps off the curb. Takes five steps across the street.

Our apartment is only a block away, but it might as well be eleven light years away. Like Epsilon Eridani.

He takes a step. Then two. Three. Another is four. Then --

The phone is a dead weight in my hand, and the sun through the curtains is hideously bright. Even now it shines, as if to say that it doesn't matter about Simon. The Earth still turns. The sun still shines.

"You must feel awful," Roxanne says.

What else would I feel. But I don't say that. She's no worse than the others. I don't blame her. I don't blame anyone.

"What if he comes out of it?" she asks timidly. "Could he?"

"He'd better not," I say. "He'll be a quadriplegic with the intelligence of a cabbage. I wish he'd died."

For a moment she is shocked into silence.

"I don't know what to say, Kelly."

I stare at the dust floating in beams of sunlight.

"Don't say anything. Just let me be. He wouldn't want this fuss. He'd want us to get back to work and get our asses to Eridani."

I have two more weeks of leave because of

the accident. I decide to go back to the Institute today. Get on with the work.

"Simon was one hell of a guy, wasn't he," she says.

My throat is tight.

"Yeah."

Simon, my tormentor muses. *Is this what makes you unhappy?*

Damn you, I scream at him. *Get out of my head!*

I'm lying on the marble flood, curled up in a ball.

You are lonely for this man? he asks, slipping in and out of my mind, palpably curious, not at all discouraged by my fury. He has found a dangling thread, and he will tug on it until he unravels everything. He tugs. I brace myself.

I am standing in a long, white hallway, just a few steps from the director's office. My freedom.

Martin yells my name from the other end of the hallway. He sprints toward me.

I curse softly. Martin has found the note I left on the fridge. Too soon, which means a scene. Right here, in front of the director's office.

It isn't Martin's fault. I know what my leaving will do to him. I know he loves me. It just isn't enough.

He stops suddenly, in front of me, breathing hard.

"Kelly. Wait."

I smile, hoping against hope to keep the conversation light.

"Wish me well, Martin. I'm off into the great unknown."

"God, Kelly," he says. "I don't believe this. You were going to stay. You said -- Kelly, you said you'd stay. Remember?"

"I can't," I say, looking at the Institute logo on his shirt instead of his eyes.

"Kelly --"

"This is the way it is, Martin."

I tell myself that I'm giving my life to science, which is true, but somewhere inside I know I'm also running away. I never thought I'd run away from anything. It's hard, finding out that I'm not who I thought I was.

"I did my time, Martin," I say, trying to turn it into a joke. "I've earned a little vacation."

"Damn it, Kelly, Eridani's a fucking one-way ticket!"

"Someone has to go. Might as well be me. I'll send a postcard back, tight tachyon beam. I promise."

I see his hands tremble. He looks as if he might break into tears at my next word. I feel the weight of his pain. It makes me want to leave even more. I hate this.

"So," he says bitterly. "What am I supposed to tell Simon when he wakes up?"

His words bite. I know that he must be desperate to say this, but it pisses me off. Tears trace quick lines down his face, fall from his chin. Suddenly my anger dies. I hug him.

"Martin," I say into his ear, "the twenty of us have been hanging out here at government expense, banging away at ancient pygmies and Amazon tree bark and classical dance and basket weaving for seven years. We keep telling ourselves we're prepping for the trip to Eridani, but eventually someone has to actually *go*. Alien intelligence, Martin."

He holds me at arms length.

"But that's not why you're going. I know how it was with you and Simon. I don't expect it to be like that with me. But God, Kelly, don't leave. He could still wake up."

His eyes are bright and full of pain.

"He won't. The doctors are just covering their fat asses by dripping sugar water into his veins. He's dead."

I kiss Martin quickly, once on each cheek and a light brush across the lips.

"Kelly --"

I shake my head to silence him.

"I had to let Simon go. Now you have to let me go."

"Kelly, goddamn it. I love you. Don't leave."

There is nothing else to say. No amount of words is going to fix what's unfixable.

"Sorry," I say, breaking my promise to myself not to use that word anymore. I mumble it again, then I pick up my bag and turn away.

I can hear Martin's breath, shallow and ragged. I hear him slam the wall with his fist.

I tell myself it will be over soon, that Martin is better off without me, that in time he will heal. I tell myself I'm doing the best I can.

In the director's office I sign my name on a lot of papers. The director shakes my hand and gives me a one-way ticket to a distant star, in a space ship that looks as much like a tin can as it does like a coffin. I can't wait to leave.

And so you left him, my alien captor says. *Are you sorry now?*

I am sitting on the ground of the domed room, looking up. I blink through tears at the bright blue in the windows. Blue that might be sky but probably isn't.

I had to come, I say. *I had to know.*

That there was intelligent life here?

That there was some reason for me to live. That I could make something count.

And have you? he asks.

Even this innocent question cannot spark my tired anger. I tell him what I've told him before.

Getting here was useless without the message I was supposed to send back.

He expresses sympathy but does not understand.

Seventeen years passed on Earth while I was in cold sleep, en route to Eridani. That's a long time for a government sponsored program, but the Institute would keep going with the status and telemetry messages my ship sent back via nearly instantaneous tachyon beam, waiting on the real goods, the the messages I would send back once I came out of cold sleep at Eridani.

Every inch of the ship was riddled with

redundant systems to insure that no matter what happened at Eridani, a message would get back to Earth. But I am certain that after I reached Eridani my ship sent back not a whisper. It wasn't supposed to be possible to silence my ship, but I am sure my captor has.

Without that message back, I doubted the Institute would be able to get the government to finance another expedition.

But surely, after centuries, Earth would send another ship. Surely the call of non-Earth intelligence would draw humanity to Epsilon Eridani again. Surely. Unless --

Unless Epsilon Eridani is forgotten. Perhaps we lost star flight technology. Perhaps the Earth is dead.

It's that last thought that turns my insides to ice.

At the Institute we publicly theorized and privately prayed that the existence of non-human intelligence would give our race irresistible reasons to go into space. Once in space, we thought, humanity would survive its self-destructive tendencies.

It was a message of hope, the message I failed to send back.

I ask him now, once again: *Why?*

He hesitates. Then, like every time before, he wraps the answer into a little package. He ties it with string, and hands it to me.

I unwrap the thought bundle with exquisite care, wanting to understand this thing that has made my life worthless. But the string falls apart in my hands, and the bundle melts into air.

It is not my lack of understanding that dismays him now. He wants my pleasure, and instead has my despair.

You do not understand, he says.

You got that right. Bright little goddamned alien.

I sorrow, he says.

I am dessert that has turned bitter. Of course he sorrows.

You are lonely, he says.

I do not respond. He has found today's key, and no matter what I say, he will use it on me. Again and again, until I have no more tears. Until I have pounded my hands bloody against the marble floor. Then he will put me into a deep sleep and I will sleep for centuries.

The room's doors have faded and the walls are smooth again. A dark fog fills the room, swelling and swirling. He is creating something. I no longer wonder if what he creates around me is reality or illusion.

Look, he says, *look what I have made for you. Look and choose.*

Around me are human figures. Naked men, each one encased in an upright, plastic tomb. Like blocks of ice. Their eyes are open and unblinking.

Choose, he says. *As many as you like. All are for you.*

Ken dolls, I say.

Not dolls, he says. *They will live and breathe.*

I promise.

Are any of them not *of your making?*

All, he replies, *all are of my making. For you. For your pleasure.*

I do not want them.

His disappointment is palpable.

None? he asks.

None.

He considers this.

There is one, he says. *One that is different. One that you may not have.*

I look around.

One of the many plastic tombs pulses pink. I walk to it and look at the man.

How is this one different? I ask.

He is the one you cannot have.

I know this is a game, but it is a new game, so I play.

I want this one, I say.

This one you cannot have, he repeats.

The next move is obvious. I take it anyway.

Then I want none of them.

He is suddenly gleeful.

I understand you, he says. *You only want what you cannot have.*

No, I say. *You don't understand.*

But his enthusiasm is undiminished. It is another key, and he will use it on me until it breaks or breaks me.

The forest of naked men reminds me of my own nakedness. I have been naked since I arrived. Then I assumed my captor wanted to study me that way. I was proud of myself when

I arrived, proud of the anthropologist I had become, that I was not the least embarrassed.

At the Institute we pushed hard at the boundaries of cultural conditioning, so we could abandon anything that got in the way of communicating with the aliens. We ate bugs and worms, we screwed each other in public, we pissed and shat and didn't wipe. Now I have no modesty.

But I do have preferences. Looking at all these men, I remember my preferences.

Give me clothes, I say.

He pages through my memories. I see patterns, I feel textures. Suddenly I am dressed in a pale blue Institute jumpsuit.

I touch the cloth wonderingly. It feels good to be dressed. Better than I imagined. I can almost believe I am on Earth, now. In a museum, maybe, just walked in. I look around at the life-like men, look for the plaque on the wall with the title and artist. There must be a plaque somewhere.

Which one do you want? he asks, breaking my fantasy.

I told you, I say. *The pink one.*

Only that one?

Yes.

All of the men vanish except the pink one. Then the translucent pink tomb disappears, and the man falls to his hands and knees. His chest heaves with deep, gasping breaths.

I walk to him. I touch his shoulder. The skin is warm, the muscles firm.

Very convincing, I say.

The man looks up at me. There is nothing behind his eyes. No understanding, no passion. I wonder if his body is an echo of my own, which my captor must now know down to the DNA. Illusion or reality, it doesn't matter. This thing is not of my race. I turn and walk away.

From my captor I feel a small rage. There is a sound behind me, like a large drain opening. Or a big sponge being squeezed. I look back.

There is a wet, red mound where the man knelt. Pieces of meat and organs slide slowly down the mound, which is a mass of flesh and splintered bone. Around the mound is a large, spreading pool of blood.

I am sorry for the creature's suffering, but only a little. We all suffer.

Now, my captor says, with a voice like honey-coated steel, *I will give you what you really want.*

The world slides away.

The ship has just woken me from cold sleep, which means that I'm at the planet that circles Eridani, where the alien message came from. The console beeps and the screen blinks, confirming that the computer has sent a message to Earth, saying that I've arrived.

My fingers fly over the control panel. I check the log to confirm that the computer sent humanity's Rosetta stone greeting to the planet. I shout commands and run all the analysis and test programs the computer can handle.

Minutes later I pause to glance out the viewport. The planet is tan and brown, with seas of green. I look for long moments. It is hard to look away.

When I get hungry enough, I eat a bit of my dwindling food rations. If I eat sparingly, I have enough food for another month. That doesn't bother me. I paid for a one-way trip.

Something nags at me. Something about the ship's message back to Earth. I check the computer log to see if the message was sent. It was. Still I am anxious, so I check again, then force myself to my other tasks.

The computer beeps again. A message from Earth appears on my screen. Acknowledgement, go-ahead: try to make contact.

The grin won't come off my face now.

I still feel odd, as if I'm watching myself from a distance. It's the excitement, I tell myself. I'm about to initiate humanity's first alien contact.

Something inside me is screaming that this is wrong.

My hand is suddenly on the switch that sends a distress signal to Earth. I pull my hand back.

"What the *hell*," I whisper, the sound of my voice loud against the close walls of the cabin.

This is not how it happened.

I reach out to touch the ship's hard metal walls. To check that they are real.

Happened?

The computer beeps. There is a reply from the planet. The computer automatically forwards the message to Earth.

I hold my breath as the computer munches on the alien message, turns it inside-out a thousand times and then spits out a preliminary translation:

"Greetings come friends union good happy."

I howl my victory cry. I can see them all at the Institute, their ecstatic grins. Even Simon smiles, from his place inside me. A new universe has just been born, right in front of me, a universe in which humanity is not alone.

Still I feel there is something wrong. What?

I curse, angry at having this moment spoiled. Everything hoped for and more, a successful mission, a diamond bright opportunity. Much better than the first time.

The first time?

The warning bell in my head is clanging. I take a deep breath, close my eyes, and try to track the cause. Like a dim star, it vanishes when I look at it, so I look to one side.

Then I remember that other time. The first time.

This is not the way it happened, I tell my captor. *You're editing my memories.*

The computer beeps. I open my eyes. On the screen is another message from the aliens. They have sent us their Rosetta stone. The computer transmits the message back to Earth as it starts to digest the alien key.

I make a fist. I bring it down on the ship's

console. The console beeps a protest.

No. This is not the way it happened. I will not be lied to. I will not have my memories changed.

I dig deep through my mind, down past my hopes of what might have been.

And there it is. The hard truth. What really happened.

I receive nothing from Earth or the planet. Hours pass, then days. I send my arrival message to Earth in a constant, repeating stream. I check every part of the ship's communication system, then all the hardware. I find no malfunction.

Five days later Earth has still not responded. I have performed every system check hundreds of times. I have barely eaten or slept.

Suddenly the ship's controls stop responding. I watch helplessly while the ship plunges through the planet's atmosphere and begins to land.

Again I try to warn Earth. The ship does not respond to any of my commands. In my sleepless, hungered state, I imagine that the aliens are monsters who crave humanity's destruction. I consider initiating the ship's self-destruct. I decide not to. I loose consciousness.

When I wake, I am in a large, domed room, with many high windows. An alien walks through my mind, trying to understand my thoughts and pleasures. He has had much time to understand me.

I am not deceived I tell him now. *Not at all.*

The ship vanishes. I am again standing on marble.

Why do you scorn your own pleasure? he asks irritably. *I give you the past you want, and you reject it.*

I reject falsehood.

He is frustrated, and he spins in my mind, a red glow. *Must your truth always be painful. Can you not allow yourself even a little pleasure?*

Not at the cost of what is true. You took everything else.

He considers this.

You are tired, he concludes.

Yes.

You want to sleep, he says.

We have come to the end of the day again. Perhaps I cannot die, but I can sleep.

Yes.

But I have not had enough of your pleasure. First give me that.

There it is, the deal. I will escape to my slumbers only after I have given him what he craves. I, the unwilling drug, bargaining with my captor for a door into temporary oblivion.

I don't want to do this. I almost remember the last time.

All right, I say reluctantly.

I promise myself that this time I will only enjoy it a little. I will not forget who I am. I tell myself that it is only for a few minutes, and only so I can sleep. I tell myself a lot of things.

He floods me.

Everything is bright.

I reach out long arms. I play in the soft clouds and green seas. The stars call to me, begging me to come join in their dance. I accept, and they fill the air around me, like fireflies, swirling and circling, becoming my halo.

I look down and laugh kindly at my mortal self, at the delightful, foolish fears I had moments ago. I am a goddess now, so I bestow my blessings upon my lesser self. I give her promises, sprinkled like fairy dust, of the wondrous things that are yet to be.

Now I see many kinds of truth. The truths mingle and frolic and twist, creating new worlds every moment. They parade like strings of diamonds. Bright as suns, deep as space.

This is what I saw in the mirror. My freedom. I could wave my hand and free my lesser, mortal self. But now I am distracted by other things that beckon with the promise of even more fantastic understandings. I fly among the promises.

I dance. I cry. I sing. I delight.

I am a rose petal, stolen from a flower by the breeze. I float slowly to the ground. Death this is, of a sort, but I understand it now; it is but one of many deaths. A truth, but one of many truths.

I embrace the fall. I open my eyes.

My captor sighs contentedly in my mind. He gives me a sleepy smile, like a man after ejaculation. A door appears in the smooth, curved wall before me. The door to sleep. My payment.

The changes he made to my body chemistry now take their due. Just as the euphoria is hard to remember after it is over, so, too, is the depression that follows. But as it comes over me, I clearly remember the last time. I sit on the hard floor. I hug my knees to my chest.

Everything I knew moments ago is gone. The words remain, but the meanings are dust. Truth and stars and freedom -- what do I have to show for these words. Before, at least, I had self-respect.

I tell myself that I will not let him do this to me again, no matter how much I want to sleep, no matter how bad I feel. I say it again and again, until I almost believe it.

I put a hand flat on the cool marble, clinging to the simple truth that I am not the floor. The world turns dark around me. I am dizzy and my stomach clenches. I know it is a reaction to the changes he made in me, that it will pass, but that doesn't help.

I want to sleep. A long, dreamless sleep.

I try to stand, to get to the door, but I am too weak.

The door opens. A man walks in. He has long, dark hair and a beard. The beard, I note with odd detachment, is new. He looks around the room, sees me. His eyes widens a little, then narrow. I'm in no condition for this game.

Let me sleep, I say to my captor. *You*

promised.

He has been asleep a long time, my captor says. *Now he is awake.*

I close my eyes and hug my legs to my chest. "Kelly?"

His voice is familiar, yet it sounds odd here. I have not heard any voice in this room for -- centuries. As he walks toward me, even his steps bring back the past. I open my eyes. He is on one knee, a hand on my shoulder.

"Kelly," he says, his green eyes on mine. "God, woman, is that really you?"

He's wearing the same kind of lightweight jumpsuit I have on. Every movement he makes seems real, true. My captor could not have shown him more perfectly.

"No," I try to say, but I have not spoken for so long that it comes out a whisper.

He stares at me, uncertain, then suspicious. He stands.

"Kelly," he says sharply, his voice slamming into my ears. When a buzzing alarm clock could not wake me, Simon could.

"You aren't real," I whisper. "You're dead. Go away."

He stands and nods. A quick nod, like he used to when we were studying together at the Institute. I know his expressions; he's remembering. He shakes his head. Just like he used to. It's very convincing.

My life's work to uncover the truth, all gone in a moment, if I let myself believe this.

Nice try, I say to my captor. *Nice try, but it*

doesn't fly. You still want to play games. We'll play games. But get rid of the puppet.

The puppet looks at me.

"You thought I was dead," it says, "Now I'm here. You're not sure it's really me. Is that right?"

I can't take my eyes off him.

"Remember Kramer's metaphysics class at the Institute," he says. "What proof would convince you that I exist?"

It is exactly what Simon would say. I am fighting my own memories. I decide to grill him. Find something that isn't Simon. Memories aren't simple; if you push hard enough, you'll find a contradiction, a crack.

Somewhere an alien, pulling strings. I struggle to my feet.

"Doesn't it occur to you," I ask the puppet, my voice unsteady, "to wonder where the hell you are?"

"Yeah," the puppet says. "Give me a hint. My ship's controls stopped responding when I reached Eridani."

"You're dead," I say.

"I see. Then this must be heaven."

I blink. I didn't expect him to say that. Is it a crack, or something Simon might say?

"Not hot enough to be hell," he adds.

It's a joke, but there's tension in his deadpan delivery. He's holding fast to what he knows, relying on the verifiable. It's just what I would do in his place.

Damn.

"This," I turn my hands out to include the room. "And you. Everything. The alien made it all. You remember the alien, don't you?"

"You bet your sweet ass," he says with sudden passion. "Where are they?"

"I've only met one."

"I hope it's small, fuzzy and cute. Are you going to introduce me?"

I smile. A hard, brittle smile and a bitter victory. Simon wouldn't say that, not here, not now. My captor is using the memories I have of the Simon who was my lover. Not the Simon who was always, first, a scientist.

You lose, I tell my captor.

Perhaps, the alien says, admitting nothing.

I decide not to play. I walk around the puppet, toward the door to sleep.

The puppet grabs me and yanks me around to face him, his hands gripping my shoulders.

"Talk to me, Kelly. What happened. Where are we?"

I am stunned at this, but it is good, very good, because this physical act, too, is something that Simon would never have done.

"Simon died," I say. "Centuries ago."

"Centuries?. The puppet frowns. "How do you figure centuries?"

I shrug. After a moment, the puppet shakes me.

"How long since you arrived?" it asks.

The real Simon would ask this. We were like that; we had to know where, how long, and how much. The question is so reasonable that I answer.

"Ten days," I say. "But each night lasts centuries. I estimate the total at about two thousand years."

He blinks; a blink of disbelief. But he's reserving judgment. Collecting data. Just like a scientist.

"If my source is reliable," I add.

"What's your source?"

"The alien."

"The alien," he repeats, his tone flat.

I can smell him now. He smells like Simon did.

Damn, I'm falling.

I try to give my voice authority. "Simon got beat up by a car. On Earth. Now he's dead."

His green eyes stare deep into mine.

"Unless he came out of his coma and followed you here."

"Not possible."

"Not possible?. He spits the last word. "Since when. Since you left. Science goes on without you, sweetheart. They dumped me in cold sleep. Pulled me out when they had experimental nerve regeneration. Experimental and *successful.* Recovery was a bitch, of course, and then you were gone. Getting approval for another ship after yours vanished --"

He looks away, lips tight.

"Why didn't you send a message back?" he asks.

I try to pull away. He grips tighter. It hurts.

"The meds," he says, still looking away, "were not excited about letting their successful regeneration case walk out the door. Rather less excited about giving me a starship. I had to be very convincing. Convincing enough that I'll be shot if I ever return to Earth.. Now he looks at me. "But I had to come. I had to know what happened."

His face contorts in fury. Not Simon, I tell myself. He grips me tighter. Shakes me again.

"To you," he says. "Why the *hell* didn't you send back?"

"I *tried*, damn it," I snap at him. "My controls went dead, too. But to hell with you. Simon is dead."

He grips my shoulders so hard that I cry out. All at once he lets go.

"You have to trust your own analysis," he says, turning away, "just as I have to trust mine."

I tell myself again that this cannot be Simon, but in my heart the seeds of doubt are questing for light.

He walks to the wall and touches it, looking up and down, trying to understand how the room is put together. I did this when I arrived, too. Does he do this because we are alike, or because the alien makes the puppet mimic me. I stand, frozen in uncertainty.

In my head, my captor speaks.

Is this not what you want?

No, I say. *I want the real Simon, not a puppet from my memories.*

But you do not seem to be able to tell the difference.

Simon is dead.

But, he says, *you are not sure.*

No, damn you.

If this man does not please you, I will remove him.

I think of the pile of blood and bones.

No, I say quickly.

Then shall I let him grow old and die, while you sleep. Will that make you happy?

He walks around the room, looking up at the windows.

Simon. The only man who could track me across a landscape of passion and reason and not stumble.

He turns to look at me, and now there are tears in my eyes. Inside me the roots of doubt are very deep. But to believe is to surrender.

I fear that I already believe.

Is he real? I ask the alien.

I know that I can trust no answer the alien gives, and still I ask. This is my surrender.

He is real, my alien captor answers.

And now there is no turning back.

Simon walks to me. I reach for him. His touch on my skin is so gentle that I crumble inside. We hold each other tightly, hungrily. We hold each other, and I rock him with my sobs. He says my name, again and again. His voice breaks, but he does not stop. He kisses me, strokes my cheek, takes away my tears. My fingers tremble as I trace the lines of his chin.

No, I say to my captor, *don't take him away. He gives me -- pleasure.*

He is yours, my captor says, smiling. It is a long, deep, satisfied smile. It might be the smile of a victor. I don't care.

Simon entwines my fingers in his own.

"You want to meet the alien?" I ask Simon. I nod at the door, behind which might be my bed, the alien, anything. "Through there."

Simon frowns. He thinks this is the same door he came in, the one that leads to his ship.

I should tell him that the alien can manipulate thoughts and objects with equal ease. I should tell him all that's happened to me these centuries.

I should tell him that he can never again be certain.

But there will time later. More than enough. And I cannot bear to part with the joy of this moment.

We walk to the door. I push it open with my free hand, my other tightly holding his. Together we walk through.

ABOUT THE STORY

This story was originally published in *Asimov's Science Fiction Magazine*, November, 1993.

Sometimes a story will seem to write itself. This was one of those stories. If I had to guess what it was about, I'd say it's about being willing to take an identity-shattering step into the unknown for the sake of the beloved.

I wrote it in a crowded office, my laptop teetering on the edge of a desk overflowing with papers and books, stealing an occasional glance across the desk at the man I loved who I knew I was losing.

So it's also a story about heartbreak and loss. Not loss of love so much as loss of ignorance, innocence, and the certainty that we know what is real.

It seems fitting that I also dedicate this story to the man who inspired it, who I am pleased to still call my friend, after all these years.